"I would do it
because I love you."

"Wow, I'm somebody!"

the Little Soul shouted,
"I'm the Light!"

"I can be as special as I want to be!"

小靈魂與地球

The Little Soul and the Earth：
I'm Somebody!

（中英雙語版）

尼爾‧唐納‧沃許◎著　法蘭克‧瑞奇歐◎圖

林淑娟◎譯

地球是最美好的天堂

中央大學認知神經科學研究所教授兼任所長　洪蘭

　　我很喜歡這本書，因為每個人心中都需要有一個神，在他失志時給他慰藉。我更喜歡知道自己肩上有個守護天使，可以指點迷津，像書中的梅爾文一樣。當然這個守護天使就是自己的良心，人必須常常和自己對話，檢視自己的信心，確信自己沒有違背上天送我們來地球上走一遭的目的。

　　這本書雖然是寫給小孩子看的，但是它意義深遠，很有啟發性，如小靈魂問：「我到了地球也是在天堂裡嗎？」神的眼睛發出一道光芒：「地球是整個天堂裡最美好的地方啊！」令我非常感動。地球的確是個最美好的天堂，假如我們用欣賞的眼光來看這個世界，我們會很感恩它提供了我們所有生存的必要條件。人類其實不應該抱怨，我們應該努力把現有的地球變成理想中的天堂，以不辜負此生。

一本值得成人認真閱讀的童書

知名圖文作家　張妙如

　　我小時候常常經歷一種特殊狀況，就是突然間會不知道自己身在何方，不知為何會有地球、有世界，為何有「我」？這種經歷隨著年紀愈大出現愈少，但那種脫離現實的感覺卻沒忘記。

　　大靈魂說自己偏食也不完美，沒有人需要當一個完美的人。我也是花了好幾年的光陰才終於明白──這世界也不完美，但它仍可以是天堂！

　　我覺得有些很好的童書不但大人也可以看，而且值得認真閱讀。

從靈魂深處去感受那似曾相識的感覺

身心靈作家 張德芬

《小靈魂與地球》是一個由《與神對話》的觀念所衍生出來的童話故事,它是虛構的,但也有可能代表真相的事實。如果你認為它只是童話故事,不足為信,我倒想問問:「相信它對你有什麼損失?」至少你在地球上的這段時間,真心相信這個故事,並且開始身體力行,我保證你的人生會變得愈來愈美好。

書中強調了「信心」的重要性,小靈魂心想事成的能力,完全來自於信心與分享,那就是把你想要的與其他人分享,這樣你就會有更多。相信嗎?這是個宇宙法則,就跟地心引力法則一樣的必然。另外,書中也提到了,真正給出愛的方法是寬恕別人。無論我們在這個世界上追求的是財富、聲望、美貌、成就……最終的目的其實都是在尋求愛,而且是自己對自己的愛。因為我們還未學會真正地愛自己,所以我們會追求別人的愛,藉由他們的愛,來找到愛自己的感覺。透過愛別人、寬恕別人,我們才能慢慢地學會愛自己、寬恕自己。

最後我要強調,這本書不是用頭腦讀的。在讀的時候,最重要的是,從你的靈魂深處去感受那個似曾相識的感覺,去體會那個「看到真理就頓悟」的內在智慧,在字裡行間去感受那個震撼你心靈深處的能量。當然,這本書與孩子們分享是最好的!孩子都是剛剛從天堂下來的,這本書多少可以幫助喚醒他們熟悉記憶中的場景。這本小書,當你再三研讀,不斷回味之際,或許也可以喚起你部分的記憶,至少,讓那種「我們都是被眷顧的」感覺,再度回到我們心中。

原諒別人就是善待自己

周大觀文教基金會董事長　郭盈蘭

傳說中有個部落沒有律法，若有兇殺案發生，部落習俗是將兇手綑綁投入大水池中，交給被害者家屬一根長竹竿，被害者家屬可以選擇用竹竿把兇手打入水底，也可以用竹竿把兇手救上來。

據研究，選擇把兇手救上來的亡者家屬較快走出傷痛，面對人生。

身為律師，我也常勸人——原諒別人，就是善待自己。真的，一切都有因果，世上沒有不能原諒的事。我們都是小靈魂，相約來到地球教室學習「原諒」的功課，感激對方給我這樣的機會學習。

別忘了，你是誰？

讓我們的靈魂在愛裡覺醒

周大觀文教基金會執行長、佛光山檀講師 趙翠慧

那一天，我的情緒跌至谷底，茫茫然走在街上，下意識走進我最愛逗留的去處──書店，一進門就被新書架上的美麗繪本《小靈魂與太陽》給吸引了。

一口氣讀完，馬上給懾住。天啊！這本書是為我而寫的嗎？我彷彿聽到那「很久很久以前」的約定在耳邊響起，想起那久遠亙古的叮嚀：因為我愛你！

今天，又見可愛的小靈魂造訪地球，帶來神的美意與開示。透過小靈魂純真的眼睛看地球，滿心歡喜地體會「愛」的真諦，學習「原諒」的哲理。

小靈魂，謝謝你！願意和大家結伴同行在靈性成長的路上。

這是每個父母都該擁著寶貝入懷說的故事

光中心主持人 周介偉

告訴我們的寶貝：

你是一個天使般的靈性存有。

「生命」是你絕佳的創造與體驗機會；

「身體」是你好棒的生活創造與經驗工具；

「滿懷信心的許願」是美夢成真的最高效運作法則；

「愛」是宇宙最大的力量，而愛的給予和接受是最美妙的體驗！

【與神對話系列】在我們讀書會開啟了許許多多人對生命與世界的視野，啟發了我們去創造與成為自己生命更偉大的版本，建議你也嘗試一讀。

　　而其中的《與神對話青春版》（針對青少年）、【小靈魂系列】（針對兒童）是絕佳的生命教育和品格教育素材，推薦給父母與教育工作者，你不該錯過。

獻給所有的小靈魂，無論他在何處。

而所謂的小靈魂，指的正是我們每一個人。

因為我們一個個都是小靈魂，被我們稱之為神的大靈魂擁抱。

但願我們每天都感受得到神的擁抱，

但願小靈魂的故事能打開我們的心，與別人分享神的擁抱。

——尼爾‧唐納‧沃許

獻給小靈魂們，你們是我們的靈感，我們的寶藏。

——法蘭克‧瑞奇歐

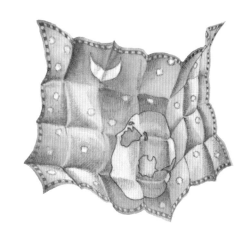

1

很久很久以前，有個小靈魂對神說：「我不想離開你。」

「好啊！」神開心地笑，「你永遠也不必離開我。」

小靈魂不明白他的話，因為這一天正是小靈魂出生的日子，小靈魂以為人一出生就離開天堂了。事實上，小靈魂已經在排隊，離「地球之門」只剩幾步路了。

「我應該感到害怕嗎？」小靈魂問。

「不、不、不！」神再次微笑著說，「這是個應該感到快樂的日子，今天是你的生日！」

「我知道，」小靈魂叫道，「可是今天也是我離開你的日子。我必須跟天堂告別了，這讓我覺得好難過喔！」

神給小靈魂一個溫暖的擁抱。「我會永遠陪著你。你不可能離開我，因為不管你到哪裡，我都會一直陪著你。」

「真的嗎？」小靈魂張大充滿希望的眼睛問。

神立即回答：「當然是真的！如果你需要我，你只要呼喚我，就會發現我永遠陪在你身旁。」

「要是事情不順利呢？」小靈魂問，他開始發抖。「我的意思是，『永遠』是好長好長的時間，要是我把事情搞砸了呢？你還會陪著我嗎？或是你會生氣地走開？」

「我當然不會走開，」神微笑著回答，「我絕對不會生你的氣。我為什麼要生你的氣？只因為你做錯事情嗎？每個人都會做錯事情啊！」

「連你也會嗎？」小靈魂很想知道。

「喔，」神笑道，「偷偷告訴你，我有點偏食，不喜歡吃蘆筍……」

連神也不是完美的，小靈魂因此覺得好多了。「好耶！你會一直陪著我，讓我好放心。這樣到地球去幾乎就像還在天堂。」

神微笑，「的確是在天堂！你不可能離開天堂，因為天堂是我唯一創造過的東西，不管你去哪裡都是天堂。」

「地球上也是嗎？我到了地球也是在天堂裡嗎？」

神的眼睛發出一道光芒。「地球尤其是個天堂。地球是整個天堂裡最美好的地方啊！」

小靈魂說：「我準備好要去了。一定會很好玩！」

「是的，很好玩，」神點頭同意。「比你想的還好玩。什麼都別擔心，即使你忘了我對你說過的話，即使你忘了我，你也會有個很特別的朋友幫助你。」

小靈魂震驚地說：「忘了你？怎麼會有人忘了神？」

「喔，」神微笑，「那一點也不奇怪。有些人會一再忘記我，幾乎每個人都會偶爾忘了我。」

「我不會！」小靈魂嚴肅地聲明，「我絕對不會忘了你。」

神說：「那很好，不過你如果忘了我也別煩惱。你永遠都有梅爾文陪著你。」

「梅爾文？梅爾文是誰？」小靈魂問。

「你很特別的朋友！梅爾文是個天使，他答應要陪伴你一輩子，所以不管發生什麼事，他都會幫助你、照顧你。」

「哇！」小靈魂叫道，「那他是保護我的天使？」

「沒錯，」神說，「所以我們稱他們為『守護天使』。現在你的守護天使已經在地球等著迎接你。」

「等一下，」小靈魂說，「你是說我有個叫梅爾文的守護天使？」

「嗯，」神頑皮地眨眼睛，「他沒辦法駕著馬車來接你。」

「喔。」小靈魂點頭假裝明白了，雖然他一點也不明白。

「梅爾文會一直陪著你，他會向你解釋所有的事情。」神對小靈魂保證，「現在你得趕快準備。你看，下一個就輪到你了！你就要出生了！」

真的耶！小靈魂離地球之門只差一步，隊伍的前面已經沒有人了。小靈魂興奮地叫：「我就要有身體了！我就要有身體了！」

　　「是的，你會有身體。」神咧嘴而笑。「好了，去吧！玩得愉快！如果你需要我，別忘了呼喚我。」

　　就這樣，小靈魂在地球上誕生了。

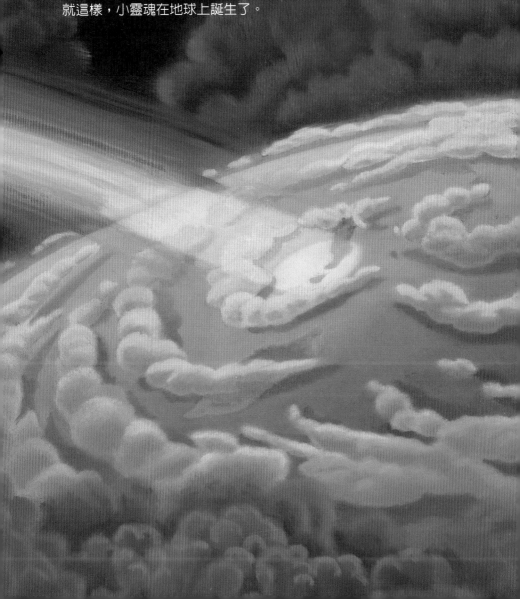

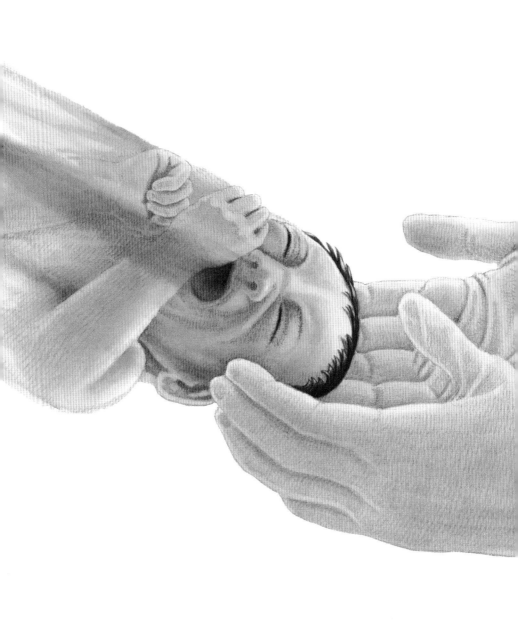

2

「哇，我成為人了！」小靈魂變成一個小寶寶後歌唱著。房間裡的每個人聽到的是嬰兒的哭聲，可是小靈魂其實在唱歌。「我不再只是個靈魂了！現在我有身體了！」

「是的！你現在是個人了！」梅爾文的歌聲自房間的另一頭加入。許多人圍繞著小寶寶，梅爾文想確定他們有足夠的空間。

就在那個時候，小靈魂聽到一個人說：「是個女孩！」其他人發出「喔」和「啊」的聲音，有幾個人甚至拍手。「歡迎妳，梅根！」其中一個人說。

「那是我的名字嗎？」小靈魂問。

「是的，」梅爾文眉開眼笑地說，「妳興奮嗎？」

「興奮啊！」小靈魂回答。「我想我是興奮的。」她有一點懷疑，因為她剛剛被一個不認識的人抱起來。

「沒有關係，」梅爾文向她保證。「她是個醫生。她只是要看看妳有多重、多高，檢查妳的身體，確定一切都很好！」

　　當醫生和護士在檢查她的時候，小靈魂想個不停。她終於問：「當女孩子好嗎？」

　　「當然好啊！太好了！」梅爾文回答。

　　「比男孩子還要好嗎？」

　　「沒有。」

　　「你的意思是當男孩子比當女孩子好？」

　　「沒有。」

　　「你的意思是沒有哪一個比較好，男孩、女孩一樣好？」

　　「我正是那個意思，」梅爾文讚許地回答。「別人的說法如果不一樣，妳不要相信。」

　　「別人為什麼要那麼說？」梅根懷疑。

　　「有些人不明白妳現在還是個小寶寶就明白的道理。」梅爾文回答。「他們長大了就忘記一些事情。」

　　「喔，」梅根了解地說，「有人才告訴過我，我們很容易忘記事情，可是我不記得是誰說的……」

　　「我以後會提醒妳，」梅爾文承諾。「現在妳必須習慣有個身體。」

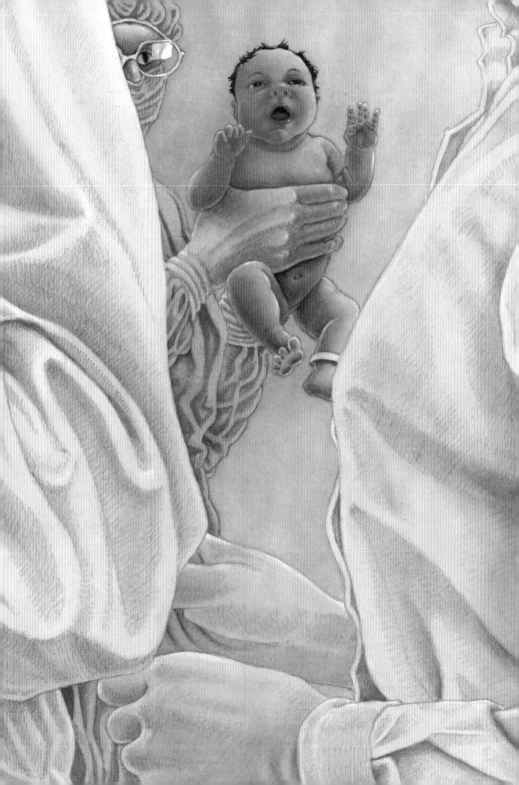

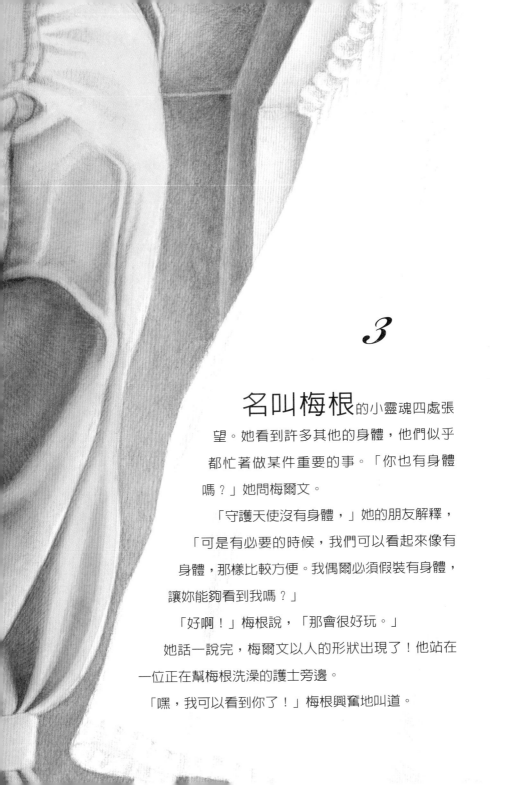

3

名叫梅根的小靈魂四處張望。她看到許多其他的身體,他們似乎都忙著做某件重要的事。「你也有身體嗎?」她問梅爾文。

「守護天使沒有身體,」她的朋友解釋,「可是有必要的時候,我們可以看起來像有身體,那樣比較方便。我偶爾必須假裝有身體,讓妳能夠看到我嗎?」

「好啊!」梅根說,「那會很好玩。」

她話一說完,梅爾文以人的形狀出現了!他站在一位正在幫梅根洗澡的護士旁邊。

「嘿,我可以看到你了!」梅根興奮地叫道。

「好。現在試著記住我的模樣，因為不久之後，妳可能再也看不到我了。」

「為什麼？你要走了嗎？神說你永遠會是我特別的朋友，每一分鐘都陪著我！」

「我會每一分鐘都陪著妳，」梅爾文肯定地說，「我哪裡都不去。可是有時候當妳告訴別人妳看到妳『特別的朋友』，他們可能會試著說服妳相信我並不存在。」

梅根大吃一驚。「為什麼？」她問。

「因為他們看不到我，所以他們不相信妳真的見過我。他們會說我只存在妳的想像中。」

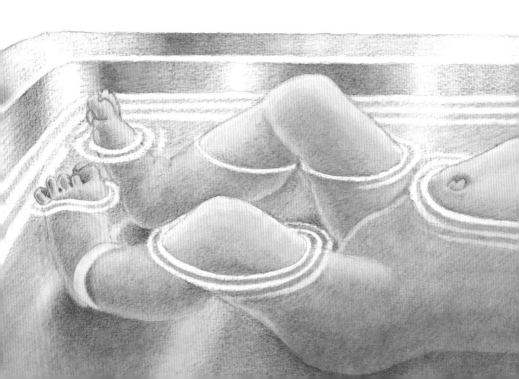

「你在我的想像中嗎？」小靈魂眨眨眼睛。

「是啊，當然啦！」梅爾文回答。「可是那並不表示我不是真的。永遠記住，妳想像中的每一件事可以真實到妳去做就會實現。」

這句話讓梅根想了好久。不過，對一個小寶寶來說，好久大約是一分鐘。然後她臉上露出怪怪的表情。「嘿！」她說，「水變涼了！」

梅爾文很快地到護士旁邊。「喔，糟了，她疏忽了。」他對小靈魂說，「她讓水涼了，沒有再加溫水。我來看看我是否能讓她想起來。」然後梅爾文對著護士的耳朵輕語。

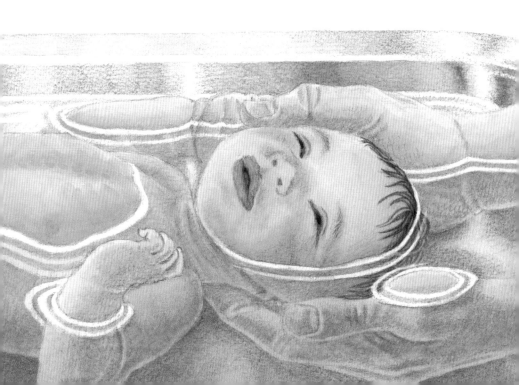

護士果真因此倒了些溫水到梅根身上。

「她疏忽了，」梅爾文再次說，「妳願意寬恕她嗎？」

小靈魂想了又想，最後終於說：「『寬恕她』是什麼意思？」

梅爾文這才想到他得教她很多事情，因為小靈魂已經忘了她為什麼來地球。她經過地球之門時會忘記以前所有的事情，甚至不記得她要求被生下來，是為了讓她體會寬恕別人是什麼感覺。

（喔，那一部分的故事你還沒有聽到，是不是……喔，小靈魂之所以要求被生下來，是因為他想體會寬恕的滋味。還沒有來到地球之前，小靈魂了解到人之所以會有生命，是為了要給他們體驗每一件事情的機會！嗯……小靈魂想要體驗寬恕，他問神他是否可以到地球體驗寬恕。可是現在，小靈魂把那些全忘了！）

「我會簡單地告訴妳寬恕是什麼意思，」守護天使告訴梅根，「不然那得花些時間來好好解釋，而妳現在正在忙。」

　　她的確正在忙。護士用一條柔軟的大毛巾把梅根的身體擦乾,然後大家都摸摸她的雙手、雙腳、耳朵和她其他的地方。他們看起來很高興,因為大家都在說:「多麼漂亮的小寶寶!她很完美!」

　　「那,」小靈魂說,「現在我有身體了,我知道我是誰了,然後呢?」

　　「妳以為妳是誰?」梅爾文問。

　　「我是這個、我是這個……」梅根指著她的身體說,「這就是我!」

　　「不,它不是。」梅爾文笑道,「我知道妳以為妳是誰,可是妳的身體不是妳,它只是妳的身體。」

　　梅根聽了愣愣地說:「嘎?」

　　梅爾文再度微笑,「我說,妳的身體不是妳,它是妳的身體。意思是說妳的身體不能代表妳,它是妳擁有的東西。」

　　「像玩具嗎?」梅根問。

　　「嗯……」梅爾文想了一下,「比較像工具,可以創造東西。」

　　「那我要創造什麼東西?」

　　「人生。」

　　「我現在就是在用我的身體創造人生嗎?」

「用經驗。」梅爾文的回答聽起來很像是某個大學的教授在講課。

「經驗什麼？」

「經驗任何妳想經驗的事，可是妳如果沒有身體，就無法去體驗。」

梅爾文懷疑小靈魂能不能了解他的話。

「我告訴你我現在想體驗什麼。」梅根脫口而出。幸好守護天使可以從小寶寶的哭聲聽懂她在說什麼，房間裡其他的人聽到的只是「哇哇」的嬰兒啼哭聲。「我想體驗溫暖，我現在又覺得冷了，我希望有人能給我一條毯子。」

你相信嗎？就在那個時候，一個女人拿一條柔軟溫暖的毯子，把小寶寶的身體包起來。

「哇！你看到了沒有？」梅根叫道，「我希望有人給我毯子，結果毯子就出現了。」

「那不是很棒嗎？」梅爾文輕聲笑，「就是這樣運作的。」

「什麼怎樣運作？」

「人生就是這樣運作的。妳可以想要某個東西，妳的願望會像妳想要毯子那樣達成。」

梅根幾乎不敢相信她所聽到的。「真的嗎？」她問，「我必須做的只是許願？」

　　「對著星星許願，願望會更容易達成。」梅爾文微笑道，「不過那不是絕對必要。只有一件事絕對有必要。」

　　「什麼事？」梅根急切地問。

　　「信心。」

　　「信心？」

　　「是的，」梅爾文繼續說，「妳要相信妳會永遠心想事成，妳要相信神一直陪在妳身邊。」

　　現在小靈魂的眼睛睜得大大的，她問出最令人驚訝的問題。

　　「誰是神？」

4

守護天使梅爾文往下看著小靈魂，露出最天使般的笑容。

「喔，我的小梅根，」他溫柔地輕聲說，「妳真的全忘了，是不是？是神把妳送到這裡，把我送到這裡，每一件事都是他安排的。」

「真的嗎？」小靈魂問，「那，他在哪裡？再跟我講一些關於他的事！」

梅爾文再次微笑。但是就在他要多加解釋神的時候，梅根被人抱起來放進某個人的懷中。

「哇！這個感覺太好了！」她開心地叫，「這樣被抱著好舒服喔！我還沒生出來之前有過這種感覺！這種舒服的感覺，不管到哪裡我都記得。給我這種感覺的人是誰？」

梅爾文回答：「她叫媽媽。」

就在這個時候，梅根感覺一隻手正在撫摸她臉頰，一個吻落到她的頭頂上。

　　「哇！這樣也好舒服，他是誰？」她叫道。

　　梅爾文回答：「他是爸爸。」

　　「那種感覺怎麼說？」小靈魂想知道，「那種我不管到哪裡都記得的舒服感覺。當媽媽抱我、爸爸親我，那種美妙的感覺叫什麼？」

　　「愛，」她的守護天使解釋道，「那種感覺叫做『愛』。」

　　「哇，那種感覺好棒。我要如何得到更多愛？」

　　「喔，那很簡單，」梅爾文說，「把愛送出去就好了。」

　　小靈魂滿臉疑惑地看著她的守護天使。「我該怎麼做？」她問。「我不知道送出愛該怎麼做，你能教我嗎？你能嗎？你能嗎？」梅根懇求，她對天使綻放她最真誠的微笑。

　　「妳知道最不可思議的是什麼嗎？」梅爾文說，「當妳對我微笑的時候，妳正在那麼做。把愛送出去就是那麼簡單，當妳真誠含笑地看著別人的時候，妳就是在把愛送出去。梅根，要常微笑，微笑是最好的禮物，每個收到微笑禮物的人都會很高興。」

　　因此，小靈魂對她的爸爸和媽媽微笑。

　　「妳看到了嗎？」梅爾文叫道，「妳的微笑讓他們感到非常快樂！」他的話一點也不誇張。梅根的爸媽心中都洋溢著喜悅，也對梅根還以微笑。

　　「哇！我對他們微笑，他們也對我微笑呢！」小靈魂開心地說。

　　「是的！」梅爾文點頭。「那是人生的另一個秘密！妳對別人怎麼做，他們會回報妳！妳真的學得很快。」

　　「很好玩耶！」梅根說，「還有別的把愛送出去的方法嗎？」

　　梅爾文輕聲笑。「有很多方法，多到妳數也數不完！」

　　「嘿，現在我有身體了，或許我能一一去做！」小靈魂叫道，「我可以花一輩子的時間學習怎麼去愛！」

　　「妳當然可以！」梅爾文贊同。然後，守護天使決定要教小靈魂寬恕是什麼意思。因為，寬恕別人是把愛送出去最好的方法。

在梅爾文幫助她了解寬恕是什麼之後，梅根依偎在媽媽的懷裡，爸爸也擁抱她、親吻她。她當下決定要原諒護士忘了給她加溫水。

當然，她還不能說話（那要等到許多個月之後，那是另一個完整的故事），所以小靈魂只能做一件事，讓護士知道梅根原諒她了。你知道她做了什麼嗎？

答對了。她看著護士，然後……

……給她一個真誠的微笑。

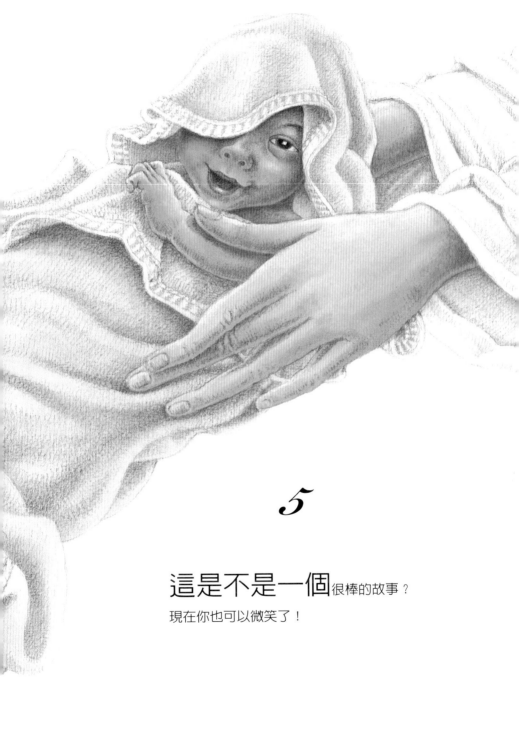

5

這是不是一個很棒的故事？

現在你也可以微笑了！

給親愛的父母和所有喜愛孩子的人

《小靈魂與太陽》的寓言故事感動全世界成千上萬人，家長和小孩都一樣珍惜它。大家對那個精采的故事的反應非常好，我們因此收到許多讀者的要求，希望我們再寫同樣的故事。人們常問：「為什麼小靈魂的探險那樣就結束了？」

喔，它當然還沒有結束，所以那些探險現在繼續下去。這本書旨在引導兒童以新的眼光去看神，去看地球上的人生和生活的目的，去了解我們可以在生活中發揮創意，去體會我們稱之為「愛」的美好經驗。這個故事也告訴小朋友，我們不僅是以肉體存在，我們除了擁有有形的身體之外，還有無形的靈魂。

如果你認為應該讓孩子了解這些重要的觀念，那麼透過一個溫馨可愛的故事來誘導他們，是最容易的方式。你會很高興你發現這本書，如同我們在製作這本書時一樣快樂。

我們發現，假如想給孩子們一些跟神、跟人與人之間的互動有關的想法時，現在的家長能找到的這類資料並不多。所以我們決定為兒童創造這個新系列的圖畫故事書，以彌補部分資料不足的缺憾。我們很高興能這麼做。

謝謝你很愛你的孩子，並把他們帶進這個故事的字裡行間。

國家圖書館出版品預行編目資料

小靈魂與地球／尼爾‧唐納‧沃許（Neale Donald Walsch）著；林淑娟譯.
   -- 初版. -- 臺北市：方智, 2014.01
      72面；14.8×20.8公分 --（心靈徒步區系列；43）
      中英雙語版
譯自: The little soul and the earth: I'm somebody!

ISBN 978-986-175-336-2（平裝）

874.59   102023585

The Eurasian Publishing Group
圓神出版事業機構
用心與你對話‧視野無限寬廣

方智出版社
Fine Press

http://www.booklife.com.tw   reader@mail.eurasian.com.tw

心靈徒步區系列 043

小靈魂與地球（中英雙語版）

作　　者／尼爾‧唐納‧沃許（Neale Donald Walsch）
譯　　者／林淑娟
發 行 人／簡志忠
出 版 者／方智出版社股份有限公司
地　　址／台北市南京東路四段50號6樓之1
電　　話／（02）2579-6600‧2579-8800‧2570-3939
傳　　真／（02）2579-0338‧2577-3220‧2570-3636
郵撥帳號／13633081　方智出版社股份有限公司
總 編 輯／陳秋月
資深主編／賴良珠
責任編輯／蔡易伶
美術編輯／李　寧
行銷企畫／吳幸芳‧凃姿宇
印務統籌／林永潔
監　　印／高榮祥
校　　對／柳怡如
排　　版／莊寶鈴
經 銷 商／叩應股份有限公司
法律顧問／圓神出版事業機構法律顧問　蕭雄淋律師
印　　刷／國碩印前科技股份有限公司
2014年1月　初版
2023年6月　7刷
The Little Soul and The Earth by Neale Donald Walsch and illustrated by Frank Riccio.
Copyright © 2005 by Neale Donald Walsch
Illustrations copyright © by Frank Riccio
Complex Chinese copyright © 2007
by The Eurasian Publishing Group (imprint: Fine Press)
Published by Hampton Roads Publishing Co., Inc. arrangement with Biagi Rights
Management through Andrew Nurnberg Associates International Ltd.
All Rights Reserved.

定價 230 元　　　　　ISBN 978-986-175-336-2　　　　版權所有‧翻印必究
◎本書如有缺頁、破損、裝訂錯誤，請寄回本公司調換　　Printed in Taiwan

Dear Parents,
and All Lovers of Children:

The parable of *The Little Soul and the Sun* has touched thousands of people around the world, treasured by parents and children alike. The response to that wonderful story has been so extraordinary that we began receiving requests for more of the same. "Why do the adventures of the Little Soul have to end here? " people asked.

Well, of course, they don't, and so those adventures now continue. The story in this book gives children a new way of looking at God, at life on Earth and its purpose, at how we create things in our lives, and at the wonderful experience called love. The tale here also shows that we are not our bodies; a body is something we have, not something we are.

If you believe these are important things for children to understand, and that there is no easier way to lead them to understanding than through a sweet story, you will be as happy that you found this book as we are that we produced it. You will also be happy to know that more of this same kind of energy may be found on the special Children's Page at www. nealedonaldwalsch.com.

There are few enough resources for parents these days as we seek to bring our children new and expanded ideas about God and about each other. So we decided to create this new series of illustrated storybooks for children as a partial remedy for that, and we are excited to be doing so.

Thank you for loving your children enough to bring them the story on these pages.

5

ISN'T THAT A wonderful story?
Now you can smile, too!

After Melvin helped her understand what forgiveness was, Meghan cuddled in the arms of her mommy, with her daddy giving her hugs and kisses. She decided right then and there to forgive the nurse for all that cold water!

Of course, she wasn't able to talk yet (that would happen many months later and that is another whole story!), so there was only one thing the Little Soul could think of to do to let the nurse know that Meghan forgave her. And do you know what she did?

That's right. She looked right at the nurse and...

...smiled her biggest smile.

Melvin chuckled. "There are so many ways, you can't even count them!"

"Hey, maybe that's what I can do while I have this body!" shouted the Little Soul. "I could spend this whole lifetime just learning how to love!"

"You certainly could," Melvin agreed. And it was then that the Guardian Angel decided to teach the Little Soul about what it means to forgive. Because, you see, forgiving someone is one of the biggest ways to give love away.

"There! You see?" Melvin cried. "Now that made them feel wonderful!" And that was no exaggeration. Meghan's mommy and daddy were both filled with joy, and they smiled right back at Meghan!

"Wow, when I do it to them, they do it to me!" the Little Soul chimed in.

"Yes!" Melvin nodded his head. "That's another secret about life! What you do to others is done right back to you! You're really learning fast."

"This is fun!" Meghan decided. "Are there any other ways to give love away?"

And at that very moment Meghan felt a hand touching her face, and a kiss planted right there on top of her head!

"Wow! What was that?" she exclaimed.

And Melvin replied, "That was 'Daddy.' "

"But what was that feeling?" the Little Soul wanted to know. "It's that feeling that I would know anywhere. What's that feeling that I felt when Mommy held me and Daddy kissed me?"

"Love," her angel explained. "That feeling is called 'Love.'"

"Wow, that feels good. How can I get more of that?"

"Oh, that's easy," said Melvin. "Just give it away."

The Little Soul looked at her guardian angel with a big question on her face. "How do I do that?" she asked. "I don't know how to do that. Can you show me how? Can you? Can you?" Meghan pleaded, and she flashed the angel her biggest smile.

"Do you know what's amazing?" Melvin began. "You're doing it right now, just by the way you're looking up at me. Something as simple as how you look at people is a way you can give love away. Just a smile from you, Meghan, is a wonderful gift that makes everyone very happy."

And so, the Little Soul smiled at her mommy and daddy.

4

M ELVIN THE GUARDIAN ANGEL looked down at the Little Soul and smiled the most angelic smile.

"Well, my little Meghan," he whispered gently, "you really have forgotten everything, haven't you? God is the One who put you here, and put me here, and put everything here."

"Really?" the Little Soul asked. "Well, where is she? Tell me more about her!"

Melvin smiled again. But just as he was about to explain all about God, Meghan was being picked up and placed in someone's arms.

"Oh, this is wonderful!" she squealed with delight. "It feels so good to be held here! It feels just like I felt before, when I wasn't born yet! I would know that feeling anywhere! What's it called?"

And Melvin replied, "It's called 'Mommy.'"

Meghan could hardly believe her ears. "Really?" she asked. "All I have to do is wish?"

"Well, it helps if you wish upon a star," Melvin smiled, "but it's not absolutely necessary. There's only one thing that's absolutely necessary."

"What's that?" Meghan asked eagerly.

"Faith."

"Faith?"

"Yup," Melvin went on. "You've got to believe that you'll always have everything you need. You've got to believe that God is on your side."

Now the Little Soul's eyes opened very wide, and she asked the most surprising question.

"Who's 'God'?"

"By experiencing," Melvin responded, sounding very much like a professor in a big college somewhere.

"Experiencing what?"

"Experiencing whatever you want to experience that you can't experience unless you have a body."

Melvin wondered whether the Little Soul would be able to understand.

"Well, I'll tell you what I want to experience right now!" Meghan blurted out, and it's a good thing that guardian angels can understand Babycry because no one else in the room had any idea what she was saying. "I want to experience being warm! I'm getting cold again! I wish someone would bring me a blankie."

And can you believe it? Just then a woman brought over a soft, warm blanket, wrapping it snuggly around the baby.

"Wow! Did you see that?" Meghan cried out. "All I did was wish that someone would bring me a blankie, and a blankie showed up!"

"Isn't that great?" Melvin chuckled softly. "That's how it works."

"That's how what works?"

"That's how life works. You can wish for something and just like 'that' you can get it."

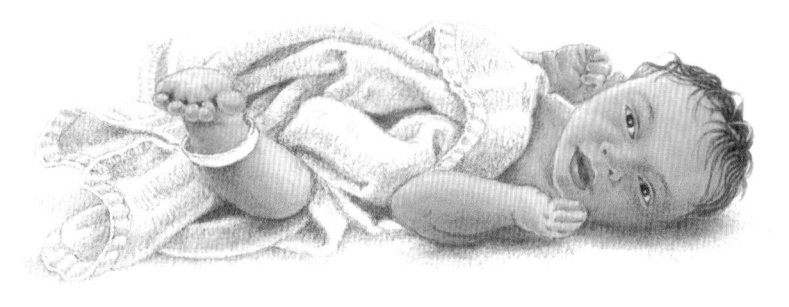

And she certainly was. The nurse was drying Meghan off with a big, soft towel, and then everyone was checking her hands and her feet and her ears and everything! They seemed pretty happy because everyone was saying, "What a beautiful baby! She's perfect!"

"So," said the Little Soul, "what's next, now that I have a body and know who I am?"

"Who do you think you are?" asked Melvin.

"I'm this, I'm this," Meghan said, pointing to her body. "This is who I am!"

"No, it's not," Melvin laughed. "I know it's who you think you are, but your body is not you, it's yours."

All that Meghan could say was, "Huh?"

Melvin laughed again. "I said, your body is not you, it's yours. That means your body is not who you ARE, it's something you HAVE."

"Like a toy?" Meghan asked.

"Hmmmm," Melvin thought for a moment. "More like a tool, to build something with."

"But what will I be building?"

"A life."

"And just how," asked Meghan, "do I build a life using my body?"

Sure enough, the nurse just at that moment poured some nice warm water over Meghan.

"It was a mistake," Melvin said again. "Will you forgive her?"

The Little Soul thought and thought. Finally she said, "What does 'forgive her' mean?"

It was then that Melvin understood that he was really going to have a lot of work to do! Why, the Little Soul had forgotten why she even came to Earth! She went through the Doorway to Earth and forgot everything! She didn't even remember that she asked to be born so that she could experience what it was like to forgive someone.

(Oh, that's a part of the story that you haven't heard yet, isn't it... well, you see, the reason the Little Soul asked to be born was that it wanted to experience what it was like to be forgiving. When it was not living on the Earth, the Little Soul understood that the whole reason anyone even HAD a life was to give them a chance to experience everything! Sooooo... the Little Soul wanted to experience forgiveness, and asked God if it could come to Earth in order to do that. But now, the Little Soul had forgotten all about that!)

"I'll tell you about what it means to forgive in just a bit," the guardian angel told Meghan. "It's a pretty big explanation, and you're busy right now."

"Are you?" the Little Soul blinked her eyes.

"Yes, of course," Melvin answered. "But that doesn't mean I'm not real. Everything in your imagination can be as real as you make it. Always remember that."

Meghan thought about this for a long time. Well, a long time for a baby, anyway — which is about a minute. Then a funny look crossed her face. "Hey!" she said. "This water is getting cold!"

Melvin moved quickly to the nurse. "Oh, my gosh, she made a mistake," he told the Little Soul. "She let the water cool down without adding some warm. I'll see if I can make her think about it." Then Melvin whispered into the nurse's ear.

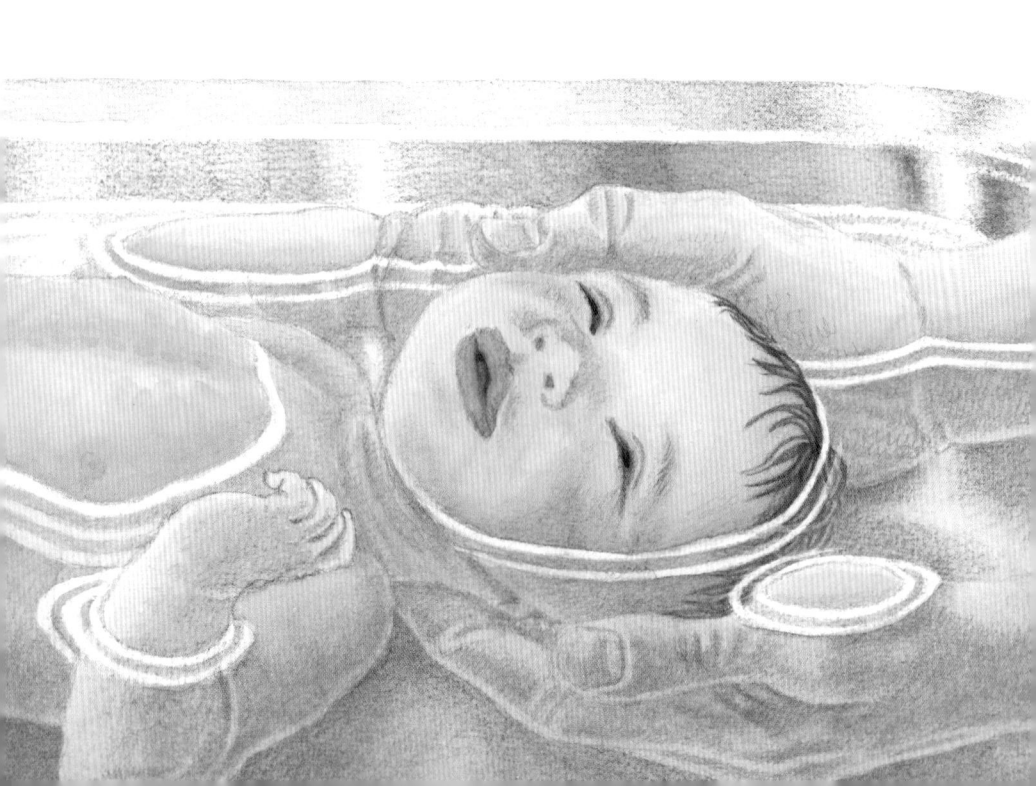

"Good. Now try to hold a picture of me in your memory because before too long, you may not be able to see me anymore."

"Why not? Are you going away? God said you would be my special friend forever, and be with me every minute!"

"I WILL be with you every minute," Melvin said firmly. "I'm not going anywhere. But sometimes when you tell other people that you see your 'special friend,' they may try to convince you that I'm not here."

Meghan was amazed. "How come?" she asked.

"Because THEY can't see me, and so they don't believe you're actually seeing me, either. And so they'll say that I'm in your imagination."

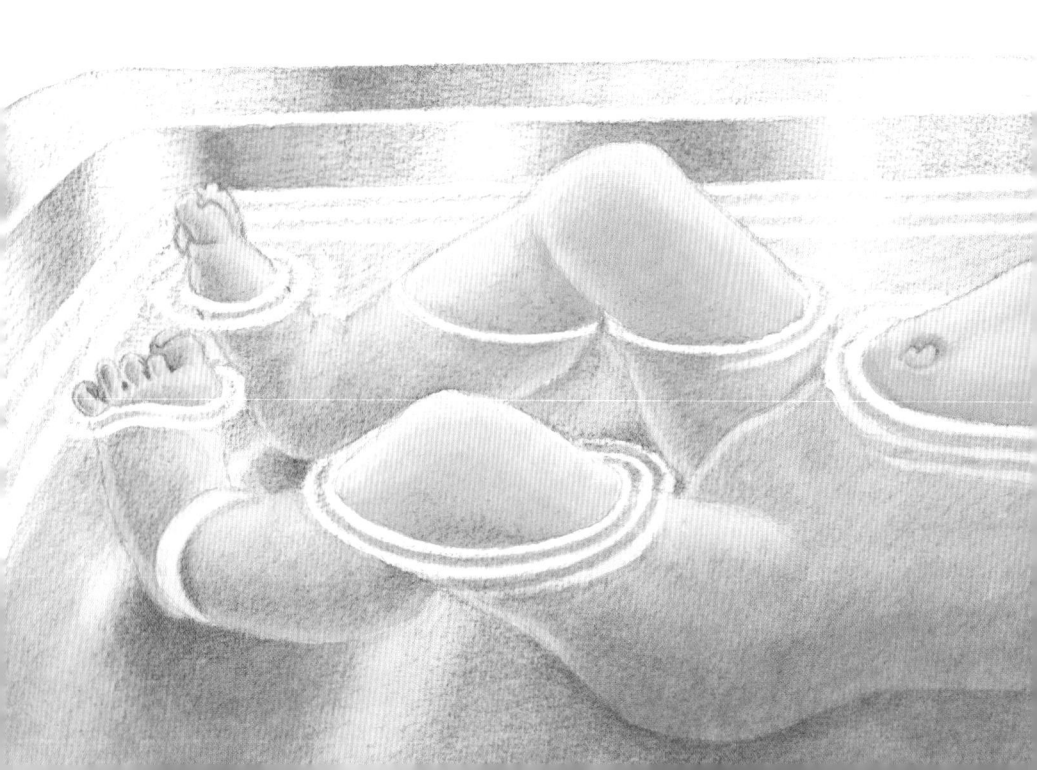

3

THE LITTLE SOUL
named Meghan looked around the
room. She saw lots of other bodies, and
everybody seemed busy doing something
very important. "Do you have a body,
too?" she asked Melvin.

"Guardian angels don't have bodies," her
friend explained, "but they can look like they
have a body, if it makes things easier. Should
I pretend to have a body now and then, so that
you can see me?"

"Sure!" Meghan said. "That would be fun."

And so, just like that, Melvin took the shape of a
person! He stood right next to a nurse, who was now
giving Meghan a bath.

"Hey, I can see you!" Meghan exclaimed.

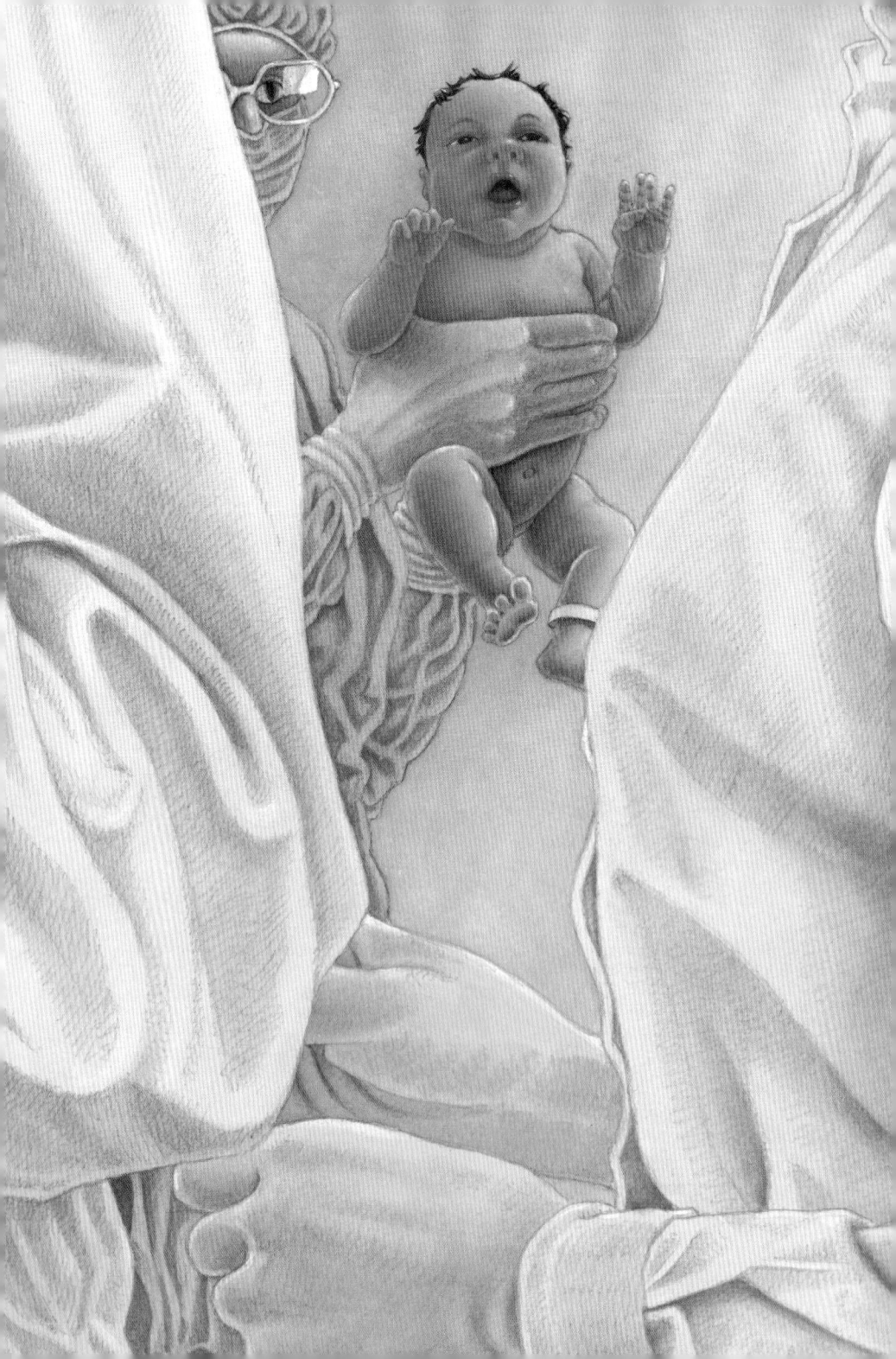

"It's okay," Melvin assured her. "She's a doctor. She's just going to see how much you weigh, and how big you are, and check out your body to make sure that everything is perfect!"

And while the doctor and nurses were doing this, the Little Soul couldn't stop thinking. Finally, she asked, "Is it good to be a girl?"

"Of course it is! It's wonderful," Melvin replied.

"Is it better than being a boy?"

"Nope."

"You mean being a boy is better than being a girl?"

"Nope."

"You mean that neither one is better?"

"That's exactly what I mean," Melvin said approvingly. "And don't ever let anyone tell you anything different."

"Why would anyone want to do that?" Meghan wondered.

"Well," Melvin replied, "some people don't understand what you know now, as a baby. They grow up and they forget things."

"Yeah," Meghan agreed. "Someone was just telling me about how we forget things, but I can't remember who it was..."

"I'll remind you later," Melvin promised. "But right now you have to get used to having a body."

2

"WOW, I'M SOMEBODY!" the Little Soul sang out the moment after becoming a baby. It sounded like crying to everyone else in the room, but the Little Soul was actually singing. "I'm not only a soul anymore! Now I've got a body!"

"Yes! Now you're somebody!" Melvin joined in the singing from across the room. A lot of people were crowding around the baby, and Melvin wanted to make sure they had plenty of space.

Just then the Little Soul heard one of the people say, "It's a girl!" and everyone "oooed" and "aahhed" and some even clapped their hands. "Welcome, Meghan!" said one of them.

"Is that my name?" the Little Soul asked.

"Sure is," Melvin beamed. "Aren't you excited?"

"I am!" the Little Soul replied. "At least, I think I am." She wondered about this because just then she was picked up by someone she didn't even know!

And it was true! The Little Soul was only one step away from the Doorway to Earth, and there was no one ahead in line. The Little Soul sang happily, "I get to have a body! I get to have a body!"

"Yes, you do!" God said with a big grin. "Okay then, off you go! Have a wonderful time! And don't forget to call me if you need me!"

And so it was that the Little Soul was born.

"Wow," said the Little Soul, "an angel who guards you."

"That's right!" God said. "That's why we call them 'guardian angels.' See? Yours is right over there, waiting to take you to Earth."

"Hold it," the Little Soul said. "You're telling me I have a guardian angel named Melvin?"

"Well," God said with a wink, "Clarence wasn't available."

"Oh," the Little Soul nodded, pretending to understand, although the Little Soul did not understand at all.

"Melvin will be with you all the time, and he'll explain everything," God assured. "But right now, you have to hurry. Look, your turn is next! You're about to be born!"

"Even on Earth? Can I be in Heaven on Earth?"

Now there was a twinkle in God's eye. "Especially on Earth. Earth is one of the most wonderful places IN Heaven!"

"Then," said the Little Soul, "I'm ready to go. This is going to be fun!"

"Yes, it is," God agreed. "More fun than you know. And don't worry about a thing. Even if you forget what I told you, even if you forget about me, you'll have a very special friend to help you."

The Little Soul was shocked. "Forget about YOU? How could anybody forget about God?"

"Oh," God smiled, "you'd be surprised. Some people forget about me over and over, and almost everybody forgets about me once or twice."

"Well, I won't!" declared the Little Soul solemnly. "I'll NEVER forget about you."

God said, "That's very nice, but don't worry if you do. You'll always have Melvin."

"Melvin? Who's Melvin?" the Little Soul asked.

"Your very special friend! Melvin is an angel who has agreed to be with you all of your life, so that no matter what happens, you'll have someone to help you."

"I know," the Little Soul cried, "but it's also the day that I'll be leaving you, and saying goodbye to Heaven, and that makes me sad."

God gave the Little Soul a big hug. "I'll be with you always. It's impossible to leave me because I'm with you wherever you go."

"You are?" asked the Little Soul, eyes wide with hope.

And God answered immediately, "Yes, I am! All you have to do if you want me is call out to me, and you'll see that I'll always be there."

"Uh, what if things don't go right?" the Little Soul asked, starting to tremble. "I mean, 'Always' is a long time. What if I mess up? Will you still be there, or will you be mad and stay away?"

"Of course not," God answered, smiling. "I will never be mad at you. Why would I be mad just because you made a mistake? Everybody makes mistakes."

"Even you?" the Little Soul wanted to know.

"Well," God laughed, "there is asparagus..."

The Little Soul was feeling better already. "Okaay! So you'll be around all the time. That's good to know. That's almost like being in Heaven."

God smiled. "It IS being in heaven! You can't LEAVE Heaven because Heaven is the only thing I ever created! Heaven is everywhere you go."

1

ONCE UPON NO TIME there was a Little Soul who said to God, "I don't want to leave you."

"Good!" God said with a big smile, "because you don't ever have to."

But the Little Soul did not understand, because this was the very day on which the Little Soul was going to be born, and the Little Soul thought that when you are born, you leave Heaven. In fact, the Little Soul was already standing in line, only a few steps away from the Doorway to Earth.

"Should I be afraid?" the Little Soul asked.

"No, no, no," God said, smiling again. "In fact, this is a day to be happy! This is your birthday!"

To all the Little Souls everywhere,
which means, to every one of us.
For we, each of us, are Little Souls,
embraced by the Big Soul that we call God.
May we feel that embrace every day,
and may the stories of the Little Soul
open our hearts to sharing that embrace
with others.

——N.D.W.

To the little ones.
You are our inspiration,
our treasure.

——F.R.

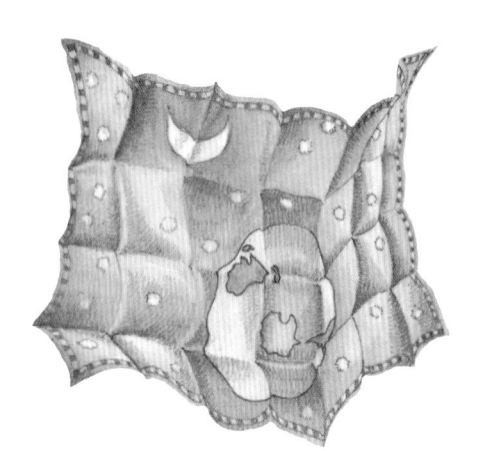

The Little Soul
and the Earth :
I'm Somebody!

小靈魂與地球
（中英雙語版）

Neale Donald Walsch

Illustrated by Frank Riccio

 "I can be as special as I want to be!"

the Little Soul shouted,
"I'm the Light!"

"Wow, I'm somebody!"

"I would do it
because I love you."